Each of Us
(And Other Things)

Ben Moor

special projects

Contents

.

Discontents

Well, you should probably close the book, put it down and go
and have a cup of tea.
Or maybe call that person you've been putting off talking to.
Go on. You'll feel better. And then it's done.

Each of Us

PROLOGUE
THIS IS MY TREASURE

After it's over, when you know it for a fact, there's that period where the world always seems to be about to break.

Time is more fragile, days are thinner.

I would sit at home like milk on a step, slowly souring in the sunlight. Friends would arrive at the flat in hazmat suits to listen to my take on the break-up, but hoping not to have any toxic doubt spill onto them and into their relationships.

I'd see experts. One analyst would invite me on walks with him and his angsthound, a dog specifically bred to sense existential crises and react with the correct levels of affection, or disinterest, whichever was appropriate.

A hypnotherapist put herself into a trance to give me her advice.

But otherwise I'd put all my energies into lethargy. I felt paralysed from the heart forward. When I left the house I imagined the people I passed on the street were marchers in a vast chaotic parade of the lonely, unaware they were even participating in a lifelong performance art piece celebrating and justifying the fundamental non-connectedness of society.

But then I thought, cheer up – come on!

A month after Radium had left, but a week before I visited the Pyre of Moving On, I went out to a party.

It's winter, a not-as-cold Sunday after a snow Friday. After Jack Frost comes John Thaw. The streets are slush gullies; the trees are rocking back and forth to keep warm in the gusts. I pass a row of bikes outside a college, fallen into an accidental orgy, wheels uncomfortably intimate with the next frame; then down a road where the paving slabs jag at critical angles and barely touch – a street of cold marriages.

The hosts are a couple of writers. He has a Saturday supplement column with a photo byline of arrogance and threat – you won't like what he has to say, and if you do he has no respect for you. She recently got back from the Caucasus and filed a story exposing the Soviet Union's Precarious Orphanages, often placed in areas notable for landslides, floods and ravenous bears and wolves. The point being that the land is cheaper there, and, well, orphans. They are both nice and welcoming to me, but they're the sort of people whose aim it is to ignite debate on subjects no one else would think debatable. Nothing one can say will finalise a point, everything bounces. Talkers.

I go to social sleep (a red standby light probably goes on in my eyes) twist away, and head upstairs. They've installed reclaimed Edwardian creaks on their stairs to make them sound more authentic. The first door was where I once stayed for a week between places – it's their unwelcome guest room, decorated in low drab, sneertones, as if it can't wait to be rid of you.

Further along there's a boy's room – he nods me in and I sit on the bed while he plays with Ruinos, the pre-damaged building bricks for dystopian landscapes. He's got a clear face, every feature seems positive, delighted to cooperate, the precise opposite of Mangold. On the corkboard is a flyer from the Large Toddler Collider, the inflatable infant accelerator at the cutting edge of high energy play. But this kid is less energetic, more considerate than you find there. Inside is always a thought, thinking its way out. We talk about his cousin downstairs, Mallory, who enters child economics pageants, declaiming Chicago School monetary theory with cuteness – "*Dumb*" he says.

His friend Joe who collects 'Heroes of Peacekeeping' inaction figures. "*Weird*" he says.

He's writing a version of the Three Little Pigs from the wolf's point of view for school; everyone is a writer in this house, it seems.

But he's also got a talent for redacting – his storybooks are blasted by black lines, barcoded to sell frustration, obscuring details too dull or too sad to know.

Unlike his parents, he asks about my wife and my work, and I explain how losing both has brought me down. And then this seven year old kid improves my life.

"What about your treasure?" he asks, "that keeps you going, right?"

"What do you mean?"

He goes under his bed, flicks out a few toys – a Despair Bear, the colouring-in-book adaptations of Gravity's Rainbow and The Atrocity Exhibition – and returns with an ex-box – not the console, just the remains of what once was a box held together with caramelised sellotape, luck and care.

"It used to belong to my dad."

On the top was written, in drop shadowed letters, 'THIS IS MY TREASURE' and, as he put it on the bed with religious hands, I guess it was. He lifted the lid and there were two things: a feather and a piece of pottery.

"Your treasure is two items – or, what, is this your dad's treasure?"

A dismissive shake of the head. "My treasure is four things – that's all you need, you can burn everything else – but I'm not going to keep it all in one place, I'm not dumb."

The feather was from a flummox, the very confused bird, native to southern Africa, which spends its entire lifespan migrating from one coast to another for no apparent reason. His uncle had brought that back for him. The pottery was from a Grecian jazz urn – did I know what that was? I did – they were the items of top-shelf ceramics from ancient Greece, portraying certain of the more physical displays of affection that that civilization gifted the world – I'd seen a few, behind pixelating glass, at the British Museum – how did he get that? He wouldn't say.

Nor would he tell me about the other two items of his treasure, or where they were. He did say his uncle wasn't at the party, as he was spending a year behind bars as pre-punishment for any crime he may commit in the future. Sensible, he thought, considering the life he lived.

Did his uncle write too? Of course. And directed. His masterpiece was a film called Sequence – a montage of montages – had I heard of it? I hadn't.

He shrugged, and gave me a copy of the in-house magazine of this house, where family members interview and write in-depth profiles of one another for themselves to read. The letters page was particularly self-involved. Then he returned to blacklining a copy of Julian Assange's autobiography, you know, for irony and giggles.

Four things. Four things a kid had, of which he kept two in a box; a box his Dad had previously used for his own treasure. What might have his been? I came back downstairs, creak, creak. I saw him in the kitchen debating the exact bottom limit of sickness where a handshake or kiss is acceptable, and decided that whatever the treasure was, like most of us adults, he'd lost it long ago and not gone looking for it since. I cheeriohed out and pushed back into the weather. I read the magazine on the bus home and remembered a plastic astronaut's helmet I used to wear when I was the kid's age, and how safe and happy it made me feel. But something else he'd said made me begin to think about Radium, and how I had to set some things on fire.

PART ONE
IT MIGHT BE BETTER NOT TO

It might be better not to tell you about how Radium and I met, but then again, I think it helps.

Newton's First Law of Sarcasm suggests that for every action there must be an equal and opposite tut, and in my job it holds true. I am a Corporate Thwart, the most loathed man in a company where colleague contempt is mandatory. My role is to replace industrial espionage – all participating firms employ a specific executive to ratchet down their efficiency; to save money on excessively competing with others, everyone deliberately makes themselves a little worse.

I send pointless memos, block innovation at every turn, demotivate the work force. I'm a shirkaholic; my unenthusiasm is infectious. Last Christmas I instigated the Secret Satan scheme where a random colleague gives you anonymous grief. I operate to a punishing nap schedule.

But this is lunchtime. I have spent the morning working on a proposal for parking tickets within parking tickets – theoretically, they're just as stationary as the car, aren't they, and therefore must be penalised? It's a good theory and I deserve a break. The canteen has its usual air of enforced inertia and my eye drifts over the meal options. Mount Mashmore, the new sculpting potatoes, with MCEschered fish, the taste of which eventually turns, subtly yet clearly, into duck. Or there's the leftovers from last night's launch party for Ventriloquism for Dummies – finger food so small as to be virtually crumbs – the race to miniaturise canapés is taken seriously here.

Our hands touch as we both go for the same cutlery-scarred tray. Radium has doubtful eyes, her clothes are scuffed all over as if they abrade against the surface of her life. I notice her neck is blotchy like she is wearing some map of the ethnic distribution of a troubled region. We both apologise with microgestures and leave the tray for the other and then both go for it again. This continues for thirty minutes – offering the tray to the other, accepting the other's offer, finding the other has also accepted, apologising and offering again.

Unfed, eventually we abandon lunch and step outside the main building. Architected by a team of hypothetical arsonists to be the exact sort of place they'd want to burn down, it is mainly painted in a discomforting tone called Migraine White to thwart productivity, but the south face is covered in a new species of algae designed to change colour over the day, following the sun. We watch a pair of bees as they consider the wall, (it was twenty past mauve), notice us watching them, and buzz off. She smokes a cigregrette, the anti-smoking aide that replaces nicotine with the feeling of tension and doom of a visit to one's family. I suck on an ennuiball.

And we sigh at the mystery and beauty of a world that had helped us find each other.

Romance had been the last thing on my mind, but the world being what it is, the last thing on my mind becomes the first thing in my heart. Radium and I compromise into love, like two people, neither of whom can quite remember the exact rules to a card game, but decide to give it a go anyway. There would be arguments, clarifications, trials and errors; but you are always surprised by how much love you can fit into open lives when you work on it together. Radium said potato, I said tomato; we decided to just agree that words with similar spellings sometimes have different pronunciations. Compromise.

Our first date. We're to meet in the Bar With Two Names. Ray enters – her silk dress is remarkable in that it intricately combines utter provocation and total surrender. I entertain her with stories that make me seem generous and unlucky; hers make her seem scholarly yet approachable. We both know how this game goes. Across the other side of the Bar That Has Two Names, her future ghost has come back in time to haunt this moment, and although she's heard all my stories before (and would have told Ray's many times) she dimples at the memory.

If some suffer from beauty-related anxiety, Radium is blessed with anxiety-related beauty. Every date she worries about, but this makes me think her more lovely.

We go clay pigeon ignoring – PULL! – visit the spin-offs from the London Eye – the London Ear, the London Nose, The London Skin and the London Tongue. PULL!

Some say chairs and tables mate for life, and I felt we were well-matched too. While it's my job to undermine others, I find Radium uplifts me.

But love takes time and time gives problems. We're on and off for good reasons. The fourth of our breakups lasts half a year. Each night I would air spoon, wrapping my body around the empty bed space Radium had left behind, holding on desperately to her absence.

The flat was intermittently full of such spaces if you cared to look – a gap where no bottles stood in the bathroom, an abandoned mug, a lone hook where coats were not now hung.

While her ghost remained at mine, she went to live for a while in South London, sharing with friends, in what was known to its tenants as the House of Reluctant Godparents, a place energised by anxiety around Christmas and certain children's birthdays. She always did anxious well. She took with her some obscure, intelligent, and sensitive books I'd given her, annotated in the margins with remarks like '*facile*' and '*really?*' for future partners to find on her shelves and be intimidated by me. In this I'd been inspired by Alexander the Great, how he constructed massive tents full of oversized furniture when he moved on, so those that later came across them would think he and his army were giants.

She, I think, actually just threw the books away; the majority of what we do is in vain. Vanity, nearly all is vanity.

We got ourselves back together soon after. And our relationship follows a predictable but difficult path. There are misunderstandings, there are explanations. The sun falls on our faces; the rain on our backs. We break up. We get back together. We snap apart at different weakpoints, fix things up. Crack under the paper, paper over the cracks.

But the only way to make this last is to wrap it in forever. Our fundamental truth was this tidal romance – we'd move in and flood with love and then go out and leave emptiness. Breakup and reconciliation was our process, and the only way to stop it was build a barrier. Marriage would be our lagoon.

I bought her an engagement void – a ring with an empty setting which was not only, yes, cheaper, but, I told her, represented the open possibility of our future together. I put it in the dish of left-handed butter, and she missed it for a couple of days (or later said she had) but when she saw it, she said, yes. To a point. At least she didn't say no. She didn't actually say anything. Again, there was an evening of silent consideration where we tried to translate the other's motionlessness into emotions. It was how we worked. Others may have thought we were weird, but I knew we were.

Our wedding day. The most typical day of my life; where there is a plan, not much goes to it. My collar is tight, a harpist faints. A reading from Ecclesiastes about how life has times and specific things happen at them. We marry, celebrate with our four friends and the next day, unproud, return to our work. Our delayed honeymoon eventually takes us to Venice, and it is here, on a water taxi on the Grand Canal, at 5.24 in the morning, as the palazzos hear the first rumours of a dawn, in a city forever dedicated to fighting inevitability, as I feel the exact weight of her head on my shoulder, that I am the most in love with Ray, and indeed anyone, I have ever been.

It is a moment I treasure.

We return from Italy. Work together and apart. A month passes and life's living resumes. But Newton's Law still operates and a tut is heading our way. We spend an evening together. We eat 90 degree spaghetti off square plates, watch a political broadcast with Mr. Low Taxes, the Tories' new hand-puppet Treasury spokesman. We make a love fraught with tenderness, and she is sleeping in the light of an aspirational candle. Her body is long, quiet, like a sandy beach on the first warm day of spring. I step outside and think. After one of our previous breakups she'd told me she faked some of her orgasms, but they weren't even fakes of her own originals, they were copied off a neighbour's, audible through our thin walls. Did that make the practice worse, or, somehow, more acceptable? On those nights, early in our coupling, after she'd fallen asleep, I would trace the lines of her veins under her skin, a long series of questions that would all lead to a single beautiful answer; her heart. But now, now, had that become a new mystery to me?

The living room. I explore the semi-dark. I ignore her ghost, sat there on the sofa. On the table, a copy of Fashion Command, the women's magazine that covers style in the voice of an Alien Emperor – "YOU WILL MAKE THE ORIENTAL LOOK FULFILL YOUR EASTERN PROMISE!!" Her handbag orb. A packet of Olops which are the bits of mints shot out to make the holes in Polos. A guest pass for the public session of the

Inquiry Into Nothing In Particular. Her. Her unrung world, and I'm not in it. Will I ever quite be part of her? Did I want to be? Well, yes, of course. But here is where I do my ultimate thwarting, the thwarting of my own happiness and that of the woman I've married.

The next morning. Cloudvertising corrupts the sky with the shapes of corporate logos. We draw the curtains. She sits beside me on the sofa, still oblivious to her future spirit, and we just stare at each other, neither of us speaking, our mouths twitching the gesture semaphore we'd used since we'd met that somehow imparts the message. Over and over. It's over.

However I had thwarted my personal life by overthinking, I still had my work to do. But that would soon fall apart too. During my time with Ray, the amount of blind alleys I deliberately sent the company down – Culties, the breakfast cereal for cults; Quaketennis, the sport played on a continually shaking court – they were bound to find something valuable at the end of one of them.

What of course it turned out to be, was the narrative gene on the 17th chromosome – notoriously a tip, full of junk DNA. Some people thought it represented the discovery of the location of the human soul, the landmark difference between us and most communities in the animal kingdom; the documented chemistry that leads mankind to create, and understand action and consequence, distraction and linearity and time and death. It's what we use to put the events of our lives into a story we tell ourselves and others. It's how we can imagine possible futures, good and bad, and what keeps us up at night. It's why we teach kids using fables. It's why we love sport, they're narratives where the ending is being determined in front of us. Humans are basically transmitters and receivers of stories; all those elements are hard-wired into each of us. And learning that changed people in different ways.

Frankly, it was all a complete accident – I'd set that team off to find the gene for gullibility – it was there somewhere, I'd been told it was, it had to be! Whatever, this and the practice of embedding moth eggs in the hems of new clothes to ensure obsolescence, and Synaesthade, the drink with the orangey flavour (not the fruit, you understand, but the colour), well, those became big wins for the company too.

Would it actually have done worse without me? Maybe. But the thwarting agreement had to be adhered to, and my brilliant success led inevitably to my dismissal.

My entire life is constructed on girders made of irony; I felt I was wearing a rosette marked 2th place in a rosette making contest.

I was fired.

Alone.

The winter party.

The kid and his treasure.

But Radium and I were only really over when I made a visit to the Pyre of Moving On, the eternal flame where one explains to a stranger the end of one's relationship before incinerating what had been left behind, and, symbolically, one's memories. You then wait to listen to the next poor soul tell their story before leaving them to wait for the next. You're only meant to remember this act of forgetting. I would sometimes return to the pyre though, stand across the street and watch the weight of others' feelings turn to smoke and drift away.

I had felt that between the engagement and the last morning we'd actually built a ruin around us, but, in another world, a better world, Radium and I stay happily together. We sing songs with our glances, our touches are ballets. Our flat fills with things that are full of us both, all angled away from the obvious but towards our hearts – a tea towel from a factory which made souvenir snow globes, a pen from a T-shirt manufacturers, a fridge magnet from a postcard museum.

Our strange combination locks us together.

Constance would be born in April; Burroughs, a couple of autumns later. Both develop faces expressing delight in a world filled with two main potentials – there were things to put in their mouths, other things to be thrown on the floor (there was some crossover in these). Burroughs would make it clear at the age of two that it would be his intention to scribble on every surface, to find a way to break every toy, while Constance would watch and gently smile as if everything was somehow going according to plan.

Radium and I fill our lives with our togetherness. We age together quietly, and one future day, we quietly slip away.

But that doesn't happen in this world.

I didn't find any of this treasure; I burned my map to it even before I'd got around to print it.

PART TWO
UNITS OF WRENGTH

I remember I'd been at Molly's. Molly is not an alcoholic nor a drug addict, but she had organised her own intervention, or what she called "A party where I am the theme". She had just wanted to talk about herself all night, and thought it would be nice if everyone she knew came over and did the same. Or, better, actually just listened to her. Not so confronty.

It was the start of what would, within months, become a fully enclosed introspection loop fuelled by Text-Witter, Friend-Acebook and barrels of processed narcissism, where Molly would talk so much about herself and the things she'd done, and her opinions, and her opinions about her opinions, that she would entirely ignore everyone else around her and eventually disappear through a hole in her own self-consciousness.

But she hadn't always been so solipsistic. She'd been out-going, she'd go out. I'd met her years before at a concert sponsored by the Department for Euphemisms (itself a euphemism) given by the Trio Quartet (they were named after the chocolate bar) and we'd gone out. She had worked for Twee Couriers, London's most adorable messenger service – freckly redhead girls in cardigans, on bikes with wicker baskets – and our paths crossed many times. I always recognised her basket from the sticker – 'Home Tracing is Killing Art.'

The homebound tube. I'm drinkdozing. Next to me, an old man smelling of dusty bacon. On the other side, a woman wearing a 'Not Pregnant, Just Overweight' badge, distributed by TfL to avoid awkward moments of misconceived chivalry. We're failing to share an armrest and, like in so many situations featuring two British people, we're involved in a stampede to get to apologise to the other; the race to sorry. And along the carriage, a woman standing at the end door. Her hair is black and long like a bad night, baggy T-shirt, skinny leather jeans, walked-out plimsolls. Her bare right foot bends at the ankle, leaving the shoe in a surprising twist, a delightful key change just at the end of an unfamiliar song.

Her name, I'd learn later, but in fact apparently already knew, was Alice. She was playing with a metal ring, the sort a mountaineer finds a use or two for. On it was looped small pictures, holes punched in them, and what looked like receipts, extracts, clippings, bits from packaging; the small pieces of card and paper that hitchhike into our lives in pockets and the bottom of bags, loiter in quiet drawers and get cleared out in the end. She was flicking through them with a record collector's fingertips continually rejecting LPs.

Her eyes caught mine and, at the speed of shame, she stuffed the ring in her bag. She got off at the next stop, with a last little look back at me at the door. It had been one of those London moments; a quick burst of nothing. Frankly I'd been still thinking about Molly's 'intervention' and if we hadn't met again the next day I would have forgotten all about it.

But we did meet – at a non-specific School Reunion, an event designed for those who don't particularly remember, or even care to remember, their teenages but feel obliged, like uncommitted Catholics, to attend something. You fill out a badge with your name and year and wait until you feel you'd done your time, not talking to anyone, and then – but there she was again. The woman from the tube.

She was surprised to find me here as it meant it really was a genuine reunion for us. She explained we had actually been to the same school. Wandered the same playing field, missed all the fun, been stairwell friends, lolloped corridors together. Had we? Alice knew things, she remembered them. But I couldn't quite place her; my memory had been semi-erased by the smudgy rubber of time and experience.

For someone who looks so quiet, when she starts it becomes clear she is a binge talker. We discuss our childhoods in our small town, boundaried by the sea to the north and unease in the future. Imagination had been our escape. I told her about my imaginary sellotape ball and how every day I'd dream it larger wrapping it in another roll of imaginary sellotape. She said she'd spent the third form accompanied by an imaginary Belgian – "He wasn't even a friend, he was an Ostend accountant in his fifties, emotionally distant, a drunkard. I imagined him smoking and drinking and being generally dismissive of my family and mates. He was just there."

Would he be part of her treasure, I wondered.

"I imagine he's dead now. So. I guess now he is."

She showed me what she'd been fiddling with the night before. Apparently a lot of people have them now. It's a year-ring. On it were all the things, all the reminders of what had made up this year for her. And by concentrating on it, by renewing the memories, by activating the narrative gene, she was confirming to herself who she was and what she'd done and her place in the universe.

"You put everything onto the ring?"

"Sure, but not everything stays; some things you realise have to come off in private."

She'd recognised me on the tube, and had been embarrassed by what I may have seen. I'd seen nothing, I said. She explained that study and contemplation of the ring would eventually lead to an understanding of the present, and so the future would seem less scary.

And what happens to the year-rings? A year-ring, when complete, is added to one's life-ring. A lifetime's snapshots, the building bricks for stories in a house of meaning. And then what? I'd learn later. Life-rings onto family-rings. Family to city, city to nation and, one day, in a hotel ballroom, would arrive the world-ring.

Alice. She'd just left a job, writing acronyms for the British Abbreviation Board, or, as it's usually known, the B. Right now she was a disclaimer writer, but she didn't write all disclaimers. Her current assignment was for a council who were getting their message across using taggers spraying public information graffiti across town.

Disclaimer writing, of course, wasn't a full-time job. She worked weekends as a hair salon stenographer, transcribing treatments and conversations.

We arranged a friend-day which would go on her year-ring, I expected. We meet at Storehenge, a shopping mall built in the exact configuration of the obelisks. We move between the retail units like bees, touching fabrics, picking up gadgets, sensing a future if we owned these things, being noticed by assistants, buzzing on. I pause at space helmets in a toy shop; at a travel agent's advertising Italy. For lunch we take a table in the food circle. I have a plate of rattle asparagus, she has a portion of paragraphi lasagne, the logical descendant of alphabetti spaghetti. She wants to know more about me. I tell her about my past work as a Thwart, about me and Radium, and although she acts interested, I get the impression she knows these things already.

There were other meet-ups, but though we only saw each every now and then – we said sometime or soon – I came to value Alice's friendship. She had the class and bearing of a semi-colon; rare, occasionally in the wrong place, but when you saw her confidence, you knew more would follow. So when I got a message from her, on the day of an awful world event, telling me to go to the Emirates Stadium, I happily went.

It was a European Nobility League group match between the Houses of Lancaster and Habsburg-Lorraine. Alice had wanted me to meet a new friend of hers called Nemo outside the ground, and I recognised him from a magazine feature written by the treasure kid's mother. Lost by his parents, he'd been known as the Boy Raised By Boys; he was almost unrecognisable from a boy by the time he was discovered and returned to civilization; but years had since passed and during the time I got to know him, only a few boylike traits remained – farts and boobs were still his constant weaknesses.

We watched the match only partially – our attention was mainly taken by the Jumbotron highlights. They'd got David Lynch to direct the in-game footage and while the contest was arid, the screen was essential. It was, frankly, the best extracurricular work by a director I'd seen since Cronenberg's notorious body-horror tinged pre-flight safety movie for Air Canada. Lynch was working live, brilliantly. He cross-mixed in the replays to go under a continuing shot of the player who had just taken part in the action so the clip looked as if they were immediately reminiscing on a narrowly missed goal chance or the injustice of an undeserved booking. The event was now not about its action; it had rejected its narrative and was now exploring sub-themes like time, self reflection, memory. Other images joined the flow, pre-recorded clips where he had followed players around, days before the match, doing pretty much nothing; shots of empty seats in the stands; vendors not vending. The mundane became the sublime.

Not many fans appreciated this radical reinterpretation of sport into an essay in anomie, but we did. We refreshed on ice lollies; he had an Orange Meander, I had a Yellow Stroll, licking quickly through the copyright warning flavour before the main taste kicked in. Nil, nil.

"And so to Destructotron!" Nemo announced. We headed out of the stadium, through a phalanx of abstract paparazzi, eager to snap Nemo but desperate to make something conceptual and angular about their shots. Some photographed each other's cameras, as if there lay the veracity of his image.

Destructotron, I found, was a tiny, below-par, Thai restaurant on the Holloway Road. So named because its proprietor always wanted one day to own an evil giant robot called that, but this place was as close as he'd ever got. Alice was already at the table, and others.

Over dinner we discuss the news that the disease that had been killing bees off, Colony Collapse Disorder, had been traced back to their sensitivity to the enormous rise in information in the environment. Once there'd just been the sun; now they were picking up GPS, texts, selfies, status updates, tweets and so on, and relaying masses of irrelevant details to the hives.

Polluting narrative was everywhere.

But Nemo is excellent. I can see how Alice would connect with him, how their life-rings deserve to link up. I watch them for some seconds smiling at each other's smiles, inspiring more smiles, performing together the geometrical calculus of love.

More year-ringers arrive. Alice wants to show me off, as if she's proud I'm part of her story now. One is an asthmatic actress who wants to break into mainstream movies – the asthmatic audience was limited and tended to wheeze through the films. Down the table Simon Anagarm, a management insultant, was presenting his theory connecting the uniqueness of every human being with the three unique elements of the opening titles of each episode of The Simpsons. Bart's writing of lines on the board – chalk – chalkdust can be used for fingerprinting, we all have distinct fingerprints. Lisa's saxophone solo – hearing – the shape of everyone's ear is different (I didn't know this – it's true). And the final shot on the sofa – it's a stretch, he says, but you watch that using your eyes, and our irises are all specific to us.

I make a contribution. I say that I doubt the universe takes the effort to hide such meanings, which buys me a round of looks that tell me I'm wrong.

The conversation turns darker. At that time, it seemed every day a new headline announced another unit's campaign of disruption somewhere in the world. Some weren't terrorists at all – one network of networkers, Friendex, hijacked planes and parked them on faraway runways, in order for the passengers to introduce themselves to each other. One of our group, Hugh, had a feeling about such atrocities. He'd survived a déjà-vu bomb attack back in 2017, so they were all slightly familiar to him. Everything was. Slightly.

It was a nice meal but I found these people a little strange; they seemed to admire me for something, or at least respect me, which unnerved me. I barely respect myself, what business did they have doing it?

After that evening I made a decision to avoid Alice, Nemo and those others for a while. I spent a week volunteering in the Lost and Found and Reduced to Fine Powder Office – the eventual reducing of unclaimed items to a fine powder had been another bad idea of mine while thwarting at Transport for London, like the 'Not Pregnant' badge – but I mainly spent my time there watching a long-running black comedy about the end of the world – the news. Each hour's bulletin changed a minor detail every time, like a game of Chinese reportage. I watched until switchoff, and the replying switchon of the little red light.

One story had been about LittleRedLightCo, the leading manufacturers of LEDs – now trying to get standby lights installed on all manner of objects when not in use: bins, chairs, shoes. Pencils. Coats. Doors. Toilets. Books. Consciences, imaginations, hearts. A scarlet galaxy at pause. The universe asleep.

But regret is the bowl in which the best fruit spoils. If I didn't reconnect with the year-ringers, would I hate myself? Would the truth about my failure with Radium be found along this path? Not necessarily as its destination, but maybe in the view through the window as I headed there? Was this what I'd been avoiding? Do I ask too many rhetorical questions? Probably. Should I stop answering them?

So I began to clip and ring the things that had escaped the pyre by luck or sentiment. A napkin from Spillages, the cocktail bar that has no level surfaces (refills aren't free; their margins are brilliant); the cardboard packet that had contained a musical zip (when you do it up it plays "A-dee-doo-da, A-dee-day"); a newspaper cutting about Ray's cousin who had just joined the Royal Canadian Mounted Air Force (they flew monstrous mutant geese). And more. And I'd go through them, and consider them, and continue. But it wasn't quite working.

I didn't feel anything here was so important.

I didn't get me.

Alice calls, we go for a drink, which she spills, and she comes right to a point, asking to move in for a while. The flat's just been me since Radium left, and her ghost only makes occasional sofa-sitting appearances now (sit happens), so I agree. And while the world outside turns increasingly unsettling, life for us settles inside there.

One night we are discussing if before the invention of the handgun, people would mime a bow and arrow to say goodbye, and she comes out and admits that the stuff up about us being schoolfriends, she'd made up. She'd just wanted to make a connection with me. Hmm.

But she's a great flatmate. I love late Sunday mornings when Alice would have a bit from each cereal packet in the cupboard, creating a cereal cocktail – Elevenses of Champions. I loved the way she pronounced escalator so it rhymed with Skeletor. That she sponsored a third world warlord – he'd write and to inform her how, thanks to her help, his ragtag militia would soon graduate to an insurgency.

But it was friendlove – I maintained a general air of ambivalence with the world in general. She wasn't mine, she was Nemo's, in whatever weird relationship they had.

An unseasonably seasonable evening. Alice and Nemo have just got in from a break in America City, on Air Quotes, the world's "safest" airline, on one of their new Lockheed-Wonka flying sweetshops, and they're unrushing from the sugar, sleeping on an argument.

I trundle.

Since she moved in, the flat has been kept in a strict mess, newspapers, food, work. She's filled in the Sudoku freestyle, bucky, jazzwise, with all the numbers akimbo. Radium's ghost stands in the kitchen, still observing, still regretting, and we exchange silent smiles.

A boom – on the next street over, a slow-motion car bomb goes off, or might have gone off weeks ago and it's just taken this long for the sound to arrive. I eat a cold slice of bootlegged pizza, the badly degraded cheese has the consistency of a sad Sunday, and pick up one of the stories the neighbourhood kids have written for Nemo's boys' group. This one is about a superhero who can shoot lasers out of his eyes, but can only use them to perform corrective laser eye surgery on others. It's good. The next one is about a magic porn mag that lets its reader enter the stories – the world may be falling apart but boys remain boys.

Especially the boy-iest.

Some unopened mail – a card from my mum who'd sent a photo of me and my brother playing in our space helmets in the garden, taken by our dad. I am wearing one of those smiles kids make, to try and see if they can break their faces. Ah.

And Alice's year-ring is sitting there at the top of a piled-up month. I know I shouldn't, but I pick it up and flick through it. There's her name sticker from the non-specific school reunion, a receipt from Storehenge. But further back there's an old newspaper article about my role at the company, about my role in the narrative gene. A mid-range photo of me and Radium getting off a vaporetto. A note with the title 'The Plan' but it's otherwise illegible, waterspoilt. And there's Nemo's – the ticket stub from the Emirates, the bill from Destructotron, a flyer for Sequence – and again, cuttings about me and my life and work, from before I met them. A stir from the hallway so I put them back down and pick up a tale about a psychic who could smell into the future. Mainly it was about farts.

When it's quiet again I step outside, looking for something to make sense of. The kerb retains a scar from when something was dropped on Radium's moving out day – one of the few physical traces of her. A couple of shards of glass from a windscreen slowly pass. The man two houses away invites me in for a drink.

'Purple Haze' is playing on the record player – "Jimi Hendrix," he observes, "His very name starts with a way to open something up and ends with a kiss." Whiskied up, we agree that the most important job in the world might just belong to whoever does the contents page for a magazine for OCD sufferers. He has a rolling mountaineering simulator in his basement – he was spending a year climbing Everest, but just a hundred foot a night. We rope together for a phase of the Khumbu Icefall.

The music is now Feedback Loop, a band whose entire repertoire of songs consist solely of instructions to the sound engineer – 'A Bit More Bass in the Monitor, Please' was their main hit. I tell him I am more of a fan of Upstairs Jazz, a sub-genre that evolved in 1950s Kansas City, where musicians were expected to play immediately on entering in venues having climbed the stairs with their instruments. The solos are breathless, fast, apoxic. I'd once seen an amazing gig at the Windows on the World. I put on a record. He relents; it's righteous.

These are weeks resembling the invisible loops etched onto a page in the effort to get a reluctant biro to run its ink; people keep trying to get things to work, but there's not much to see.

Month four of the crisis. The concept of wrength is popularised. Everyone knows the situation is wrong and getting more wrong, but exactly how wrong is it? Appalling events are measured in units of wrength and judged against one another so they can placed on a generally accepted spectrum of the awful.

Alice leaves a kitchen table note, suggesting I meet the year-ringers at a hotel. Across the street, a playground designed for, and solely populated by, child bullies. They're all sneering at each other from the edges, all too afraid to go on the swings, worried for the consequences.

The hotel is busy. One main room is hosting the Beekeepers Association Annual Ball – they fill the dancefloor with extraordinary wiggly moves telling each other how to find the bar and the buffet. This year's Queen sits in the middle of the throng, engorging herself with the group's offerings.

Down the corridor, there's a meeting of the National Distrust, dedicated to destroying the nation's least historic buildings so future generations can learn nothing about them.

But in this room there's everyone from that night at Destructotron. And about a hundred more.

And there is Mangold – the man whose concept this all was. The ring-leader. I watch him from fifty feet away, talking to Alice and Nemo, but instantly I see he has an air of genial clarity about him, as if his moment was calmly welcoming him into the future. His face is large – not ugly though – it's as if his genes hadn't quite got themselves across in his parents' features so wanted to underline their points in him. But his voice is assuring, controlled, intimate, pulling space towards it. Alice points me out, he approaches, and, with quarter-to-three arms, he welcomes me to the year-ringers in a hug, hard and full. I may not quite understand his world, but the embrace claims me. "Belong," it says. "Remain."

There's a table with Rabelaisian petits-fours. Glasses of distraction alcohol. When the time comes, Mangold takes to the stage and electrifies the crowd with his speech. They wave their current rings in the air and can't wait to connect them all. He calls people up one by one, and it's quite something to watch them place their own lives, along with those of other followers, on the world-ring. To connect with those who believe the same as they do. Most make eye-contact with me on their way back down the steps, seeking me out as part of this day of theirs, a cameo in their stories.

A week later there's another incident. Central London is hit with Difficulty Sleeping Gas, a toxin designed to make the next few nights long and uncomfortable but not much more than that. It's low level terrorism – actually not terror even, it's inconvenience-ism – but it has an effect. We're losing the plot. England is ending slowly, politely, like a shared pudding no one can quite bear to finish, as taking the last piece would just be unseemly.

I can't sleep so, like many, I explore the early hours. These nights the air is so sireny, it feels that half the country is on fire. I guessed the Pyre of Moving On would begin to expand, randomly burning things around it in flames of change. The fire brigade has decided to station an appliance there full time now as a precaution, and I recognise one of the firemen from my schooldays. He had been a soaker as a child, the evil twin of an arsonist – impulsed to cover things in water – and now here he was, living his wet dream. What with cutbacks and mergers, each fire engine is also now a mobile library, and while standing by to extinguish the flames of dead passion, he's also checking out Gone Girl for a young Mum. I walk on.

I scuttle round the edge of a massive protest by the Civil Sarcasm Movement, and head through Chinatown. When I'd first moved to London I remember being surprised it was named because of its population of Chinese people rather than the fact that, as I'd expected, the buildings were made of porcelain. I'd said I'd meet Nemo at the Museum of Incomprehensible Art, a place that catered to those with brows so high they barely fit through the door. He said he'd found an answer and wanted to share it with me.

It was a hastily organised late-night opening for Bulow/Gregory, the poet who wrote about sculpture, and the sculptor who interpreted poetry. They'd lost a son early in their marriage, and ever since had taken out their creativity on each other. For their entire careers they'd been basing new pieces on each others' previous work – it was pointless to wonder which came first, the poem or the sculpture.

I walked around 'Poem Seventy-nine,' read 'Sculpture Eighty' and although it was exhibited as incomprehensible, I felt I could see what was going on. They were completely double-helixed together in their lives and art, and by now there was no point in untying them. They were part of each other.

And it was there, in a gallery dedicated to the ungraspable, as safe a place as any during that year, as the world slipped towards disaster like an unguided teacup about to miss the edge of a table, as I wait for Nemo, a guy who stood for very few of the things I knew or cared about, and for whom I was apparently part of a plan, that I took and was taken by something.

All these moments, all these details, all these times when the narrative gene was trying to find me my story; they hadn't been random. They'd all been pointing towards a simple truth.

The human soul isn't actually something that resides inside your mind or on a strand of DNA. It's not in the things we have, or what we leave behind. Everyone's soul lives in each of us, invisibly in the stories we tell and are told by others about us.

Because yes, our lives entangle, yes we seek connection.

We don't know how our stories will end or where they're going to take us next, but all our stories should be treasure hunts. And once we find something valuable, there's no point in burying it for only ourselves to enjoy; the richness of a soul is in how much it shares its wealth.

And for each of my own treasures – my astronaut helmet, this time, Venice – they weren't just about me; there was always someone else. My Dad, who gave me that helmet because he knew how I would love to see the earth from space; these friends, trying to find their roles; Radium, leaning next to me on our honeymoon, also watching a day begin.

Because it's people, not things in a box or on a metal ring, not even the memories.

They, and not me, they are my story.

And they are my treasure.

I think I hear Ray's voice whisper my name and I look up. Nemo's arrived. And he's with Alice. And I spot a few more of the year-ringers around the place.

They're smiling at me, and I don't know why, but I get the feeling that something's about to happen.

Please Wait Here

A man pauses in a country house and tries to think of a question. He looks around at beautiful art, exquisite carpets and furniture, but they are not what stills him. He stands for a moment and sees the house as a place where time lives along with the people, an unmentioned guest. He imagines the place in the long centuries before it contained a building, through ice age and forest and clearance. Then on through its construction, the family's grand residence, these recent years. And further into the future. One day there will be ruins, moss and grasses. A squirrel may someday scamper this corridor. Nature will reclaim the land after our short lease.

He takes it all in, but maybe takes in too much. Maybe as he breathes in the present, he also inhales a whisper of eternity.

Peter Farrow is a writer of ephemera, of things that don't terrifically matter, of the sort of work that doesn't change your life but has a value in its immediate moment. He writes questionnaires. We find him now in a meeting with people at Ickworth House, just outside Bury St Edmunds in Suffolk. Silent, but sitting beside him, is his professional partner and girlfriend Catherine Spendling. Inside her she has an answer to a question he is yet to ask, but it is not the one he would hope to hear.

"Yes, of course," he says, in reply to something he's just been asked by another person in the meeting. "Well, shall I just set out my way of working? OK. So essentially, we have categories of questions which a good questionnaire will mix together. Most are going to be straightforward; I mean, the user should simply need to observe and report: e.g. 'Q: How do you know this is a Library? A: There are books.'

"Right, yes you're right; that was an easy one. It was meant to be. But take it from me, the writer of that question would have spent hours studying the room, simplifying the information, clarifying it, distilling it. Look at the words used: 'you' 'know' and 'this' – anyone should be able to answer it, so long as they are in the right space at the time.

"OK, you're following me?"

Yes, naturally, they are following him fairly easily, as he has said nothing particularly challenging up to now. He sips his instant coffee and spills a column of drops down his V-neck jumper. Catherine observes this, rolls her eyes thirty degrees, glugs from her mineral water bottle and makes another mental step towards her emotional destination. When Peter looks to her she smiles though, hiding from him her feelings – her apparent confidence in him inspires him a little.

"But our work goes deeper. You see, we often throw in a tougher Need To Asker. Sorry, right. That's just our jargon. It's a question that may include a difficult word or concept. What you'll find is that often one user will ask their teacher about it, and the information will pass around the group. This encourages talking and a bit of reliance on the adult leader which tends to ensure discipline. An example? Ooh, well if you have to ask me, well that shows you understand what I mean. Haha. You see, you want to expand your own knowledge? I'll leave examples for you later.

"Then there's a Counter."

He looks to Catherine to see if she might give an example. Again, all she does is offer a diluted smile, granting him conditional courage to continue, but no actual assistance.

"Um, so 'Q: How many vases can you see in the room?' No, it doesn't have to be vases. Anything, really, that there are *some of*. Right, so this category demands silence and a full looking around the space, all around, above eye level, all over. An ideal total for the correct answer lies in the range of whole numbers between five and twelve as, apparently, and there's been actual research on this, counting in that zone represents the average level of interest for most 10 year olds – four is too simple to count and they lose concentration if they have to go too far over ten."

The others in the room are aware it's odd that Peter pronounces the letters 'Q' and 'A' but say nothing. One person notices the tension between him and Catherine, but also says nothing at the time. She will mention how moody she seemed to her colleagues a few days later, over a lunch of re-reheated soup.

"Some like to include a Sketcher question requiring a modicum of artistic ability – I always think this is pushing it. If a client wants one I insert a picture of an item and get the child to draw a missing object onto it. Girls tend to get these questions right; Boys always draw the same thing. You can guess what that is."

They can. Of course they can.

LATER

Although they don't live together, most days Catherine comes round to Peter's flat to work at the large dining table in the walk-through area just next to the small kitchen. None of the rooms in this place make much sense, as though they've been placed where they are randomly, but this one gets the sunlight and you can fit in a table. Despite being in absolutely no danger of floating away, its surface is weighed down with laptops and coffee cups, piles of books and magazines, post arrived and post to go. Each has their demarked space, which, even when they were new lovers and would tenderly get up and massage the other's shoulders, kiss the other's neck, they were careful not to disturb. He is mentoring a young questionnaire writer called Chris. He comes to the flat too and sits at the same table as him and Catherine and gets on with his work, occasionally raising his head to ask a question about this or that question; 'Should this be an Asker?,' 'How long between Counters?' Peter regards himself as a hands off mentor, believing the mentee must himself be active in getting the instruction they need – a signpost doesn't shout its directions to anyone passing, it simply points the right way when examined. So, essentially, the table currently hosts three distinct office spaces. It's a fairly large table.

Chris has come from student journalism and is working on a questionnaire for a proposed Exposition of Experimental Drugs (Expot 11) that the experimental pharmacy industry wants to put on later in the year – if they can prove there is an educational content in removing oneself from one's face, they can get a grant, and Chris has to find that content.

Today he is using Campbellase, an inhaler which makes everything seem to go all tartan. They have discussed how tartany the table is, how Scottish cows might produce tartan milk and the way he's looking at the rubber plant, Peter suspects Chris might be making a breakthrough in the application and usefulness of tartan chlorophyll.

Catherine has let Peter take the lead on the Ickworth questionnaire, and she gets on with her commissions. She spends much of the morning scowling at her laptop, and tapping her teeth with a pen. Over the course of their affair, from laying out the dimensions of their passion, to building the trust and furnishing the comfort, Peter has learned that while it's never the right thing to do to ask her how she is, it's also never the right thing to do to ignore her. He spends most of the day thus quandaried and hopefully strikes the right balance between showing he cares enormously and showing doesn't care in the slightest.

He should get on with the questionnaire. But where to start? What should be Question Number One? Maybe he should start with the entrance hall and The Fury of Athammas. Julie Andrews always says starting at the very beginning is a very good place to start. But surely there's a pre-beginning that's an even better place? What about the stucco friezes around the Rotunda – might there be a question about them? Something to do with the sports they all seem to be playing? But then he thinks back further – is there a question to do with the approach to Ickworth that takes in the overall aspect? Or going further back – something to do with the car park? The front gate? What the questionee did before making their trip? The origins of universe?

This takes two days of thinking and doodling. Peter is paralysed by the possibilities of the first question – where do the answers need to begin? What is there about the stillness of Ickworth that has taken all the activity from him? A place where there so much had been going on throughout history, so much wildness, so much living in the moment. But on his visit it had seemed ambered, eternal. At twelve on the third day he looks at the chair that had just been occupied by Catherine and sees her absence and thinks of a question: 'Q: What belongs in this space?'

He finds her in the kitchen, a room the size and smell of a slice of burnt toast. She is plunging the handle of the cafetiere, causing it to squeeze out an accidental geyser of dotty coffee onto the work surface.

"I've nearly finished the coffee – will you get some more?"

He says he will, but over the next few days he doesn't. He believes this act of non-coffee buying represents a small defiance to her and her evident success in doing something that is not writing the first question of the questionnaire. But it doesn't represent that really. Each time he makes the coffee he uses half of what's left in the jar, making more watery coffee, or, later, more coffeeish water, each time. He becomes Zeno's Barista. The courage his defiance affords him is outweighed by the weakness of the brew, and, in fact, a week later it is Catherine who breaks and buys a new packet. Except she doesn't break as such: she is unaware of any such defiance and just wants a nice cup of coffee.

But while he observes this small surrender (which is, of course, nothing of the sort), her success in working away while he remains solidly not, he regards as winning in bad grace (but is nothing, again, of the sort). Her commissions are now coming in regularly; he hears her end of phone calls – deadlines, fees, wordcounts – while his life is dominated by both ends of nothing.

Chris next goes on Elegance, and drifts around the flat dressed like a Restoration Libertine with all the linguistic flair and romantic malice he can muster. "If science be the food of love," he declaims to the plant he previously accused of being tartanised, "experiment on."

Peter informs him that quote is riffing on Shakespeare, half a century and more before the Restoration. Chris responds with a diatribe about how time further past is still part of time past, that's it's arrogant of us to think what went before was solely meant to be part of our lives, and history moved with our ancestors the way it moves with us into the future. And he says it so elegantly that Peter finds it hard to disagree.

And meanwhile time, within Peter and without him, passes.

EARLIER

Each room at Ickworth is stunning, but every chair, every clock, each table is covered in a dust sheet, as though this is a house occupied by the ghosts of cliché who want their nonliving space to resemble them. It is out of public season, it doesn't open to the public until March. Alternatively, it is high season for privacy; in March then, the quietness closes.

He is allowed to lift a cloth here and there, half-expecting to find something spooky underneath; a skeleton of a clock, say, with just its bare workings and none of the outside adornment. But no, they are magnificent, if stopped. Their movements do not move; they are waiting for the eyes of the year to fall upon them, for them to be the answers to internal questions of beauty and history, and eventually, his questionnaire too.

He takes photos, stands in doorways as his users will, at thresholds where new information will come upon them and new facts would be recorded.

LATER

His block continues. He can't talk to Catherine about it as, by raising it in conversation, by defining the void, it will become more real.

He goes to The Bar With Two Names which is where he'll find like-minded and like-working other ephemerists. In one corner are the ingredients writers, a couple of them jokily reading the labels on their beer bottles while another sits sheepishly. A contents page writer he knew when he worked at The Observer in the 90s is on a date with a surprisingly tall Japanese girl. She writes the boards in office building lobbies, listing companies and floors as palindromic haiku – they'd been wanting to meet for years, and it's only ever been likely to happen here in The Bar That Has Two Names.

He orders a generic gin and takes a seat over with Sally. She's copyreading tickets for a train operator who want their customers to pay more attention to their terms and conditions.

"They're the two words I dread the most now. I mean who cares? Do you care? Does anyone in here care?" Her partner, Jane, writes Terms; Sally used to do Conditions, but had a notorious burnout during the 2008 financial crisis when it seemed nothing she had written had made a blind bit of difference. He explains his problem with Ickworth and shows her the guidebook.

"It's glorious," she says, correctly. Each page she turns inspires a new glint in her eye, the paintings, the furniture. He explains how he had seen it all out of season when even the motion brought by visitors walking through was absent. Catherine had been there too, but now she's distracted by her magazine work and he can't get going on it alone. Sally listens and offers nothing helpful, but in the telling he finds himself almost inspired – sometimes all it takes is talking about a process for the process to get moving. Sometimes inspiration follows explanation.

He is able to step outside himself and see such moments for what they are, tiny parts of a progression. Like one of the sped up segments in a documentary about things growing and dying, time can be manipulated but only relatively. It was a revelation to him when it was explained that the reason everything looks so fast in those films is that the camera is, in fact, itself going very slowly. The technical term for this is cranking, he understood; it can produce the comedy of a Benny Hill routine or the beauty of the Milky Way passing over a canyon. But when he is the camera, and it is his work he is observing, moving slowly the way it is now, all he can see is unprogress.

EARLIER

In the Silver Room, upstairs. He takes pictures of the pictures of the admirals on the walls. What seas they saw, he wonders, smiling at the pun he has made that he dare not share with anyone. Catherine hates puns.

She says, "Look – a tray of cold fish." He joins her and looks at the display.

He says, "They're beautiful. We could put in a counting question about them." He hopes to get her agreement, but there are not many things they will agree on anymore. She smiles a deceptively friendly smile and looks beyond him.

"You're missing my point. They are cold fish." And steps towards the next room.

The lady showing them around pauses, acknowledging the tension.

From over her shoulder, speaking as if her words are butterflies. "It was a fairly obvious point." He likes butterflies and therefore doesn't get hurt by them.

"It was. Thank you."

He lets the words flitter off and returns to taking a photo of the tureen with the ounce on the top and wonder if the questionnaire users might find such an object more interesting through form or function. What is the animal on the top? What food would be kept in it?

At the end of the tour, the lady asks, "Are there any questions you'd like to ask us?" Catherine has returned to silence; Peter tries hard to think of something good.

LATER

This stillness he had caught from the house is what still afflicts him. Chris experiments today with Boxon-30, which gives the user the impression they are trapped in an invisible box, and seems to be performing street mime. Catherine types away in the sunshine slanting through the blinds, her foot tapping the floor to the music in her headphones. But Peter sits still and think of the chairs at Ickworth. The way nobody sat on them anymore. A chair becomes a better chair when it remembers the shapes of those who have sat on it, but now these chairs were there to leave impressions instead on those who viewed them.

They lived in the time zone beyond the rope, the place where what was then could be observed by what is now. And now would ask the reconstructed then about then, and hopefully gain reflected insight into a construction of now. This can't be the only function of the past, though. History isn't just there to be quarried and refined to enrich the present; it has value in itself. Peter just had to find the value that would make his first question a winner.

It's day seventeen of the inertia. He sits on the fourth side of the table today as if a new point of view will provide inspiration. On his laptop, he flicks through the photos he took at the house. He does this every day. He knows these images almost too well, their framing, their dutching (another camera term, meaning an unhorizontal shot), the bad exposure on certain ones, a half smile on Catherine's face caught just before she makes her comment about the fish.

Peter has begun to enter Ickworth in dreams and moved not normally, not walked about; he has flipped albumatically from Kodak moment to Kodak moment, simply transported himself to the next room or significant feature in jumps. As though the information around the photos has nothing to offer him. All there is in his dream-Ickworth are the questions he has, in order to find the question he has to ask.

So he finds a photo and examines it.

Q: The Stairwell. There are numerous circles in this space. How many can you see? Count the circles in the wall, in the girders in the glass ceiling, the irises of the eyes of those around you, buttons, coins, the circles in which your life is taking you and others. What is the total?

Another photo:

Q: The Drawing Room. Stand in the corner of this room. What time do the clocks say? Draw your concept of time in the space provided.

Another:

Q: The Dining Room. List all the foods that have ever been, and will ever be, eaten here. Who had the best meal and what did they have?

Another:

Q: This is a Library. Ask yourself what the books here should tell you? Is there a good answer?

Nothing is working.

Meanwhile Catherine has been working on a questionnaire for a woman's magazine about the ends of relationships. They discuss whether this form of question and answer document is theoretically a *survey* (a word Peter utters in disgust) since at the end the data is collated into 'Mainlies' to provide a pat analysis. He tests her eyes to see if the mention of surveys brings anything up. Does she still think of Simon, he wonders. She wonders why this matters to Peter, as things like that never mattered to Simon. She also now wonders, "What is Simon up to these days?" and emails him later that afternoon, while Peter maintains his constant level of furious inactivity.

As he looks around he takes everything in. He is not to be interrupted as he absorbs the atmosphere, shoots a few last photos, jots an occasional note down. If Zen Buddhists intend to be one with the universe, at perfect peace with all the knowledge of the cosmos, in his small way he is doing much the same thing – only with the intention of extracting just the right atoms of knowledge and shaping them to his will. Does that give him a Buddha complex?

They say friendly goodbyes. The wind picks up to blow them on their way. Peter takes another set of photos at the front of the house. Catherine plunges her hands into her pockets. "It's round."

"It's a rotunda," Peter answers, with some accuracy.

Catherine is on her way to the car now, but mutters the following just so it's audible and the point hits: "You're rotunder."

An example there, of Catherine calling him fat. She does this a lot. He is fat these days, but denies it to himself. He notices the swift degradation of conversation from a statement about the building to physical insult, and a pun. Catherine does not hate all puns, as Peter believes; she simply now hates his. A more sensitive man would have understood this, and taken it to represent a clue as to the decline of the relationship. What might cause such coldness between partners? Does time decay everything, or is there a place for conservation of affection, even when the habitability of the pairing is so doubtful? Catherine thinks not; Peter is oblivious.

In November 2006, after a wedding party, nearer the Suffolk coast, at Yoxford, he had seen a pair of shooting stars and felt the urge to call her, even though she was still with Simon. Simon was a survey writer for a government agency and was doing well at the time. But Peter was up and coming in the world of questionnaires; he was beginning to be spoken of in the same breath as Matt "The Falcon" Warrender, the legendary Australian whose questionnaires at the Millennium Dome were the one of the few true success stories of that whole sorry affair. Peter and Catherine had met at the inaugural Latitude Festival, also in Suffolk, that Summer.

He had made the call at three in the morning, ostensibly to commentate on the historic meteorite shower he was convinced he was witnessing, believing this to be a romantic event that would bond them forever, but the call had involved long periods of awkward silence, punctuated by his occasional assurances that another one would appear any second and her pleas to be allowed to go back to bed. He eventually relented, and has not seen another shooting star in all the years since.

So much of life is waiting, thinking, wondering. Hoping that the universe is just about to provide a good answer, all the while trusting we're asking it the right question.

LATER

It's a week further on. In her mind, Catherine has left Peter, but needs to keep coming to the flat to finish the work she has already lined up before ending the business and romantic partnership. This is how she sees the world – it's a series of answers she gives to it, rather than the other way round.

She receives a survey about her dreams from the British Insomnia Society. If her dreams were sufficiently interesting would she mind donating any she could spare to the sleepless? The following day one arrives from the Right Shoe Board ("How would you describe the difference between the right and the left shoe in your favourite pair?").

Peter notices the amusement they bring her. He wraps up a comment in a mumble, which she asks him to repeat. "He's trying to get your attention."

Catherine looks up – this is just about the first thing Peter's said in days. "Everyone gets surveys. It might not be him."

Peter, is on a roll. A roll of despair. "It is him. It's obviously him."

He is sure Simon is doing this. The surveys display his trademark wit and panache, qualities his own questionnaires have when at their best. But only when they are written. Unwritten ones have no discernible qualities.

Each survey delivers a fresh new smile to Catherine's face as she fills them in across the table from him. Once complete, she envelopes them, puts them on the pile of neat, complete post, and returns to her work, fanning herself with a bank statement, gulping bottled water, then playing a word concerto her laptop keyboard, a virtuoso pianist, tapping out brilliance all day, while he still sits and stares into a deepening screen-sized abyss.

Chris, glumming on Mopex, stinks around the flat like a crime in a carpark.

The next day's survey is from the Ghost Defence League. "Neither haunted nor unhaunted;" "Very possessed by evil spirits" and "Not at all willing to be exorcised" are just three of the categories. The following day Peter intercepts one from the council regarding local parks, which clearly isn't from Simon, and feels embarrassed.

The blank chasmic screen stares back into Peter and he is pretty sure he can his soul in it, receding away into the dark.

Catherine leaves Peter a letter. It talks of the things he has stopped talking about and is generally kinder than it needed to be. But as it's placed next to the pile of other mail, he puts it into the post without ever reading it.

It's for the best.

Sometimes no answer is the right one.

Catherine doesn't come to the flat the following day or for the rest of the week, or indeed ever again, and so it's just Peter watching Chris trying desperately to sum up his experiences with Anecdotol (a drug that enhances storytelling abilities) without comparing it to other incidents in his life. Peter has, by this stage, had more than enough of Chris. His theoretical encouragement of the younger writer has been defeated by the annoyance caused not only by the series of thoroughly distracting drug experiences, but by his frustrating ability to actually write good questions about them. If misery loves company, work avoidance simply requires a smoking buddy.

He tells Chris to leave, and, on the doorstep, wishes him well. As Chris walks about for the next few days, goes into pubs and meets people on buses, traces of Anecdotol still in his bloodstream, he tells numerous strangers about Peter and his unbegun questionnaire, and he does it so delightfully, and with such amusing and acutely observed moments, so lively does he tell the tale, that he makes many new friends, one or two of which will last a lifetime.

So that's Peter, all on his own, day after day at a large dining table, thinking about how he might begin to ask the visitors to Ickworth House about what they are experiencing, while unable to answer similar questions of himself.

One night, a night when there are shooting stars, unseen by his sleeping eyes, the night before Ickworth opens for the year, he comes up with the perfect question in a dream. He is unable to recall it in any intricate detail later that morning, but what he writes is pretty close. As though a foundation stone has been laid, he continues building his questionnaire from that point, and, while not writing the immaculate first question would forever bug him, when, eight years later, he meets up with Catherine and Simon and their children at Ickworth, questionnaires in hand, she agrees that it wasn't too shabby.

By this, she means it was pretty good.

In the Dining Room, one of Catherine's children asks Peter what the word 'Baroque' means, and he looks out of the window and catches sight of a still squirrel, paused on the centre of the lawn, trying to remember something important.

Anew

We look at each other,
We move together,
We kiss.

And for that moment,
Everything is stopped.

The inexorable progress of things
Becomes suddenly very exorable.

A flower,
Tilting back and forth in the breeze,
Remains forth.

A football floats in the air
Like a distant frozen planet.
The children below it are awed astronomers,
Ants in amber.

A flipped coin stays undecided
Between heads and tails,
Heads and tails.

A woman in a warm bar,
Gesturing to her girlfriends the size of something,
Is stuck like a street mime out in the cold.

Airliners at take off lean into the air at tilted angles;
Those landing dip onto the ground like stone divers.

The long air of an old room
Retains the wood sound of a ticking clock.
Not even sound waves are moving now.
The light is held.

The international flow of capital pauses.
The sea stops.
Email stays in its position.

Political movements
Reach political standstills.

And then we spin,
We move apart,
We look at each other.

And then the world is begun again.

Anew.

Saint Valentine's Day 1999

The Specifics

You want me to tell you
What I love about you.
But in specifics.

I head for the corner,
Think,
And return.
I say,
How about I tell you in English?

You smile and I start.

Well, it's not your general hair,
It's your bad hair.
Not your teeth,
But that one tooth.
(You know the one I mean)
Not all your skin,
The bits where you've written things.
The back of your hand -
I know this part well,
I love it specifically.

It's not how you generally look,
But the specific way the early sunbeams
Make your skin so clean and new.
The way you get your things to match.
The way you usually choose
Entirely the right shoes.
But sometimes not,
And the days when you don't,
That's a specific sweetness too.

I wouldn't say
It was the way,
You talk generally.
No.
The specific voice you use with me
When you tell me about your make-up.
That's a thing.
The way you take foreign language words
And make them your language.
Our language.
It's the way you say my name
When you're feeling love.
You say it in a whisper.

It's not the general food we eat
It's the tiny things.
The flecks of pepper you've put on something hot,
The sugar grains on something sweet.
The clouds in your coffee,
The fourth cheese on your pizza.
The glass of wine that was just the thing you needed.

It's not all the times we have together.
It's things like the cartoony face you make
When you dance to a song you know.
The skip you walk with in parks.
The smile you show shop bookshelves
When you're looking there for something specific.
Maybe you haven't noticed me
Noticing that.
But I have.

You're the way I see the world now.
Specifically words and shapes,
Melting on condensated windows.
Specifically lonely gloves
Dropped on wet winter pavements.
Specifically toysize jetliners, bound abroad,
Skimming between the distant towers of this city.
You're the sweet feeling of warm puddings
On cold days.
Of iced drinks
On days of boiling sun.
The feeling of arms and legs and lips and hips
All touching.
Cherishing.

Is that enough?
I ask.
You smile and nod in that specific way
I love

And you say,
Now tell me in French.

Saint Valentine's Day 2001

Of Course Any Other Three Moments Would Do Just As Well.

This is me:
Two thirds up a tree you told me to climb.

If you loved me you would, you said.
I do so I do.
It's a strawberry day when clouds haven't mattered
And the grass has been our friend all barefoot afternoon.
We have chained daisies, peeled apples, shooed flies.
I reach up for the further branch.

This is me:
Entering the water, a freeze grabbing my feet.

A November stroll down a skyworn beach
Long full of nobody but then us;
Our running, our hope.
The wind ripping sheets of seaside into our eyes
And we leaned like cliffs into the gusts.
You said, let's go paddle.
I wade on towards you.

This is me:
By the mantelpiece.

You said I'd be fine.
A party just uncorked and bubbling up.
We came together and are mingling away;
Spirits in a cocktail.
With people I like but who know you better.
I'm stuck for someone's name and you see this.
You pause and hold back.
With lost puppy's eyes I look lovingly to you.

These are me.
Climbing, paddling, struggling.

And these are you.

Your face, washed clean with sunlight,
Yelling me higher, higher.

Your hair, thrown into a rolling halo,
Your eyes open, your skin fizzing.

Your hand hiding a laugh
You'd hate your friends to hear.

These are three moments.

You begin to climb the tree.
You take my hand.
You step over and save me.

Saint Valentine's Day 2003

Sartorial Mastermind

If you were alive in the 1970s you probably played the board game called Mastermind. There may be an app for it now. There's an app for everything.

The box had a besuited and bebearded older man, sat in front of a shiny table, all his fingers touching in the universal position suggesting consideration. And he's accompanied by a seeming exotic Asian young lady, glamorous in a futuristic white dress. (I say exotic, but as pointed out on the show *Better Off Ted* there are proportionately way more Asians in the world than Europeans, so, mathematically, who is the exotic one really? Eh?)

Look I'm getting distracted. If you know the game, skip the rest of this paragraph; if you don't, read on. The idea was that one player (the Mastermind) hid a row of four coloured pegs behind a screen and the opponent had to match the exact colours in the exact order by placing other pegs in holes and offering them as a guess. If you got the right colour peg in the wrong place, the Mastermind setter popped a smaller white peg into a hole next to the row as a token of encouragement; the right colour in the right position was rewarded with a black peg. These pegs were smaller and fiddlier and although they seemed to tell you that you were on the right lines, it took quite a bit of thinking to work out which of your own pegs was correct. You got ten attempts, and the game would end either when you cracked the Mastermind's code or the game slipped off the table, accidentally or by tantrum, sending pegs everywhere, their destiny to be either swallowed by the dog or trodden on when you weren't wearing any shoes.

So the game was fun. It combined two of my favourite things: a puzzle with little plastic objects and the opportunity to test everybody's patience. But however enjoyable the game was to play, I had always loved the photo on the box best. The Mastermind (there might have even been a TV advert with him on it) just looked like the classiest guy in the world to me in rainy old Whitstable. He had cufflinks, he might have even had a digital watch made by Texas Instruments. But it's his expression that intrigued me the most – just what was this man thinking; just how had he placed his coloured pegs this time; his fingers were so considery, I bet he knew he'd win. Was there a high stakes Mastermind circuit in the casinos of the world, played in penthouses by the jet set, for stakes of up to a million dollars at a time. Would they use pegs? Or something more dangerous?

Now in 2004 I had been doing fun things for The Idler magazine for a while, writing about the stuff that fills the happier, lazier bits of the world. I'd written for them a piece about collecting single lost gloves I had found on the street during a winter when I was coming to the end of a relationship (Glove Story). I had also written a piece about board games which they used in their spin-off publication called Pilchard Teeth. Also, they threw amazing parties, in those days at a place called The Tardis by Farringdon Station – don't go looking for it, it's not there anymore. So when Tom Hodgkinson, The Idler's editor, a man inspired by willful acts of leisure and with a gentle spirit as great as his talent as a writer, said that the ICA had suggested they host an Idler event themed around games and playing called Counter Culture, and would I sort of do some of the organising, I placed my pegs out there. Yes, I said, I would.

So I made a video mix of vintage board game TV ads downloaded from the internet, and this was in the days before EweToob, so it took some actual effort. I got hold of the brilliant Mike Leigh, co-founder of legendary early 90s club night The Double Six Club where you'd choose a game from a menu and it would be brought to your table while you'd drink cocktails and listen to easy listening music; these were the first days of irony. Mike wasn't available for the live event so I transcribed the phone call, including all the ahs and ums, and I read it on the stage with the superb poet Clare Pollard taking Mike's role. It was weird, it worked.

Mike and Fig (his Double Six partner) lent us some games for the night and a rolling championship was initiated; challenges for the crown had to be accepted on any game and whoever was wearing it at midnight would win a big prize. This turned out to be an artist called Susanna Edwards who had been to another event in the building, but had found ours to be way more fun; she and a friend eventually used their prize (a really cool game that featured electronics and safe cracking, I think) as barter to pay for their taxi ride home. Adam Buxton was on the bill and was great; we also ran a Swap Shop where you could bring in a game you no longer wanted and trade it.

There's a point. I'm coming to the point.

But another part of the evening involved a live game of Mastermind, only with the twist I had always thought the guy on the box would use. Coloured plastic pegs? Pah! What if, I thought, what if the man on the box is actually *always playing* Mastermind. What if he stops a guy on the street – this might be like one of those epic American short stories where it's all a metaphor for heaven and hell and he's probably the Devil – and says if you can guess the colours of my vest (except he wouldn't say vest), pants (again, not pants, Americans have different words for everything) and socks (socks is actually OK), you get these four black pegs (which are probably his family's souls or something). Maybe that's why his fingers are in consideration pose in that photo: "Yeah, I'm playing Mastermind right now! Under my stylish suit! And only I know it!"

So for the ICA evening, I dressed wisely. I had on a yellow T-shirt, blue pants, one sock was green and the other was red and made sure they weren't outwardly visible. I printed up tons of game sheets featuring a blank man with spaces to colour in the four items of clothing, and distributed sets of coloured crayons and pencils. When people got a right colour, wrong place, they won a white mint imperial; a minstrel was the prize for a correctly placed guess. And it was fun. It was easy to learn and play, and got people sharing crayons and competing with their guesses. I had to do a mini-flash to prove the winner had cracked my dresscode (nice), but I think it was late enough for people not to be too upset by seeing non-matching socks. There was a good prize too, but some people made deliberate wrong guesses just for the sweets. Oh, and there was also a prize for the best bad board game idea. I forget what won, but, come on, it can't have been better than Sartorial Mastermind.

You can create your own game, of course. It's so easy! All you need are coloured crayons and paper, mint imperials (or other white sweets), minstrels (or other darker sweets), underclothes of guessable but varied colours, and a sensible outfit to wear on top to keep them hidden. Be warned that you'll have to show off at least a bit of your garments at the end, though.

And at the back of the book is the image I distributed for colouring in. Please note the hands with three fingers; I am a lousy drawer. Maybe you should make your own. Probably better if you do.

I ran another game at Bethnal Green Working Men's Club in 2009 during one of Robin Ince's School for Gifted Children nights as part of the London Word Festival. This was more of a science themed evening, and there was a prize too for most imaginative colouring in. Some of the best entries are up on my website, along with a downloadable blank figure and the text of the interview with Mike about The Double Six Club.

Ah, I just thought. A good way to end this piece would be by saying I am in fact playing Sartorial Mastermind at this very moment, and I welcome your guesses, dear reader.

I should then put my fingers together in contented consideration and smile enigmatically. Yeah. Nice.

I'm just going to go and change now.

Please wait here.

A Bit at the Back of the Book

So this is like that extra they cram in on a DVD where they all say how everything happened to be, and factettes get revealed. It's ever so skippable, but I guess you might like to know a little about stuff and stuff.

Each of Us. My last solo theatre piece was *Not Everything is Significant* in 2008 and it sometimes takes a while to get something new together.

Five years is ages though. Sorry.

How I work on my shows involves transcribing long lists of images and moments and jokes and lines of dialogue. Most of them are made up, but some come from real world observations. They're then stirred together in my brain and on bits of paper and typed up, examined, edited, re-written, thrown away, recovered and shuffled around. And then, somehow, they tell me what story they're all part of. That's when the work begins.

I first performed scenes of what is now *Each of Us* on 25th May 2010 at a friendly music night called Totally Acoustic Live. They consisted of the section where the narrator meets Radium in the canteen, and part of the bit in the flat with the slow motion car bomb. The opening prologue with the party and the kid and the ex-box was first performed at Interrobang?, a groovy performance and spoken word club, on 27th September 2011, and the whole piece was read to an invited audience at the Leicester Square Theatre on 15th December 2012.

Excerpts have been sent out to members of my mailing list over the last couple of years too. They would have read all the different titles the story went through: *The Options, This is My Treasure* and *The Earth From Space* were all tried on and discarded.

There've been re-writes and edits along the way, and there may be still. What with print deadlines, the version in this book might not be exactly the stage script as performed at the Edinburgh Fringe in August 2013 and afterwards – apologies if a good line isn't in this book, or a bad one is.

On stage, the piece is played in a weird gallery-like space. The stage furniture is a bench and at the back of the space is a reproduction of an amazing painting by the artist Kerry Brewer. Her work offers the briefest glimpses into the shadows and twists in our reality; you shouldn't think of them as pictures but as spells. Her online gallery is www.kerrybrewer.net.

The awesome score was by Simon Oakes and Mark Moloney and was played live along with the performance at the 2013 Latitude Festival.

Erica Whyman not only directed the piece with her usual magic touch and made the stage show fantastic to perform, but she also suggested essential re-writes and clarifications. Malcolm Rippeth lit the show moodily and ingeniously, and Kat Hoult was fantastic managing and operating it every day.

The story itself was inspired by a few things I've grabbed from the world these days, from people's self-obsessions to bees and little red lights. Sorry if it feels a little melancholy – I thought it was an interesting direction to take it in. An early draft was even more downbeat and Ballardian. Different people find different ways to describe the ending – it's sort of a Rorschach Test of the soul; the narrative gene in active mode, if you like. I have a feeling as to what happens next – there are clues in the text – but it's nice to leave the moment as it is, hanging in time.

If you're interested in future live performances of this or any of my other pieces, the excellent Tom Searle now puts together tours for me. His website is located at www.showandtelluk.com and he has stacks of great people doing terrific shows.

Please Wait Here came about through the brilliance of Catherine Hemelryk and Hayley Lock. Their project (Now That Would Be) Telling involved them creating new works inspired by and placed in various National Trust and historic buildings. Hayley would reinterpret the stories of the place and works of art already there, and sneak in wonderfully warped versions of what she'd found in response. It was fun.

Other writers were also commissioned to write short pieces of fiction in inspired by these locations all over the country, and a meta-narrative involving meteorites and mirrors came together. I was thrilled to write about my experience of Ickworth and the way history and time and silences contribute to such visits to the recreated past, and how they stay with us.

If you're near Bury St Edmunds and get the chance to visit Ickworth House, do go: I promise it will be more lively than poor Peter found it.

Other texts from the project are online at www.issuu.com/nowthatwouldbetelling

Three Poems. I'd write love poems every Saint Valentine's Day, and would either sit on them or send them to those I loved. *Anew* (the one from 1999) kind of inspired a moment in *Coelacanth*, and then there's tree climbing as well in the one from 2003. I guess I continually steal from myself; I re-use and re-work. I am bad. I'll now go and sit in The Bar With Two Names.

Sartorial Mastermind. Pictures of previous examples of colouring in and a digital copy of the blank figure to print up at home can be found on my website under Games. You have to provide your own crayons, sweets and prizes though. Happy playing!

Oh and this is the photo I mentioned in *Each of Us*. Man, I loved that space helmet.

Oh and yes, if you would like to know more, please check out my website at www.spesh.com/ben or go ogle me and you'll find my stuff.

You can join my mailing list by following the link there. You'll get offers and news from me but only fairly infrequently.

I'm not so into the pestering.

My previous book is small and yellow, called *More Trees to Climb,* and was published by Portobello Books in 2009. There's some quotes about it on the back cover, and it's still available at all good bookshops. It's not available at any of the bad ones, but they could probably order it for you. I sell it on my website and will do you a signature and dedication if you buy it from me. And you get a free badge. I know, right? There's also a CD of incidental music and songs that developed from my shows, by Simon Oakes and numerous talented collaborators. It's called *Almost the Right People* and it's altogether lovely.

So one final thing to fill out this page; a poem about afters:

Just Desserts

A sherry one
Is very fun.
But a rum trifle
Is a trifle rum.